PUFFIN BOOKS

The Robot Dog and the Big Dig

Frank Rodgers has written and illustrated a wide range of books for children: picture books, story books, how-to-draw books and a novel for teenagers. His work for Puffin includes the highly popular *Intergalactic Kitchen* series and the picture books *The Bunk-Bed Bus* and *The Pirate and the Pig*, as well as the best-selling *Witch's Dog* titles. He was an art teacher for a number of years before becoming an author and illustrator. He lives in Glasgow with his wife and two children.

Frank Rodgers

The Robodog and the Big Dig

PUFFIN BOOKS

PUFFIN BOOKS

Published by the Penguin Group
Penguin Books Ltd, 80 Strand, London WC2R 0RL, England
Penguin Putnam Inc., 375 Hudson Street, New York, New York 10014, USA
Penguin Books Australia Ltd, Ringwood, Victoria, Australia
Penguin Books Canada Ltd, 10 Alcorn Avenue, Toronto, Ontario, Canada M4V 3B2
Penguin Books India (P) Ltd, 11 Community Centre, Panchsheel Park,
New Delhi - 110 017, India
Penguin Books (NZ) Ltd, Cnr Rosedale and Airborne Roads, Albany,
Auckland, New Zealand
Penguin Books (South Africa) (Pty) Ltd, 24 Sturdee Avenue,
Rosebank 2196, South Africa

Penguin Books Ltd, Registered Offices: 80 Strand, London WC2R 0RL, England

www.penguin.com

First published 2002
5 7 9 10 8 6 4

Set in Times New Roman Schoolbook

Printed in Singapore by Star Standard

British Library Cataloguing in Publication Data
A CIP catalogue record for this book is available from the British Library

ISBN-13 : 978-0-14131-031-2

Chip, the robodog, loved being a
dog.
He loved chasing his tail, digging,
fetching sticks and playing ball.

He also loved going for walks, but he knew that he wasn't supposed to go out by himself.
Dogs had to be *taken* for walks.

Rex, the dog next door, had just been taken for a walk – so Chip wanted to go for a walk too.

2

He fetched his lead. Surely someone would take him out?

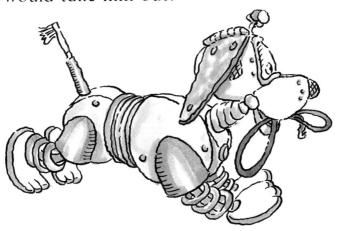

But everyone was busy. Sue and Gary were playing a game on their computer.

Mum was working on a new invention.

Dad was up a ladder in the garden, hammering.

4

He stopped and looked down at Chip.
"I still can't believe we have a dog I'm not allergic to," he said.

"If you were Rex I'd be sneezing myself off this ladder right now. But you're not, so I'm perfectly safe!"

Chip shook the lead and dropped it by the tree. "Woof!" he barked in his tinny, crackly way.

Dad smiled and shook his head. "Sorry, Chip," he said. "Too busy. I'm building a cat-proof nest box for the blue tits."

The robodog looked up. Two blue
tits were flying round the tree.

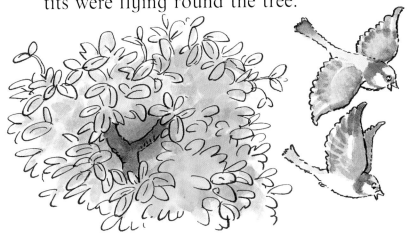

Their song was like tiny hammers
on an anvil. "Tee-tee, tee-tee,
tee-tee!"

Dad grinned.
"They're getting
impatient," he
said. "I'd better
hurry up."

Chip wandered away.

This was no fun.
No one would
take him for a
walk.

Just then he saw Selina, next door's
cat, slinking along the garden wall.

The robodog suddenly felt jealous.
Selina could go anywhere she
wanted. She didn't need a lead.

Chip frowned.

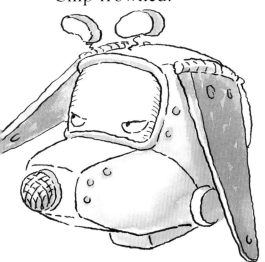

Cats had
more fun
than dogs!

9

He came to a decision. He was
going to behave like a cat. That
way he would have more fun.

The robodog
began
bouncing on
his springy
legs.

With a final, huge BOING

he soared into the air and landed on
the wall beside Selina.

The cat arched her back. "Sssss!"
she hissed.

Chip arched his back too. "Sssss!" he replied.

"Yaowl!" yelped Selina in surprise and jumped off the wall.

"Yaowl!" repeated Chip and followed her.

Selina didn't like this game. She
scooted across the lawn and leaped
into the tree.

"Miaow!" she complained.

Chip ran after her and …

BOING!

He sprang
into the
tree as
well.

Selina disappeared among the
branches and Chip began to look
for her.

Poking his nose
through the
leaves, he came
face to face with
Dad.

14

"Miaow!" said Chip.

"Aaah!" cried Dad in fright, and jerked backwards off the ladder.

Reaching out in panic he grabbed hold of the nest box to stop himself falling.

He swung in mid-air for a moment before ...

CRACK!

... the nest box came apart in his hands. Down he went ...

and landed, sprawling, on the grass.

"Tee-tee! Tee-tee! Tee-tee!"
cried the blue tits as they
flew off in alarm.

Chip jumped down from the tree to
check that Dad was all right ... just
as Sue and Gary came running up.

"Did you hurt yourself, Dad?" they asked anxiously.

Their dad shook his head. "I'm fine," he said, getting to his feet.

"But I've broken the nest box."

He looked at the robodog. "Chip was in the tree. He said *miaow*."

Sue and Gary stared. "Why did you do that, Chip?" asked Gary.

The robodog sniffed. Wasn't it obvious? He was being a cat, that's why.

At that moment, Rex poked his head into the garden and Chip's ears swung up. A dog!

Chip knew that cats and dogs didn't usually get on.

He arched his back and hissed. Rex backed away, confused.

Chip looked into Rex's garden. Mr and Mrs Minted, the snooty neighbours, were there with Selina. They had a large silver cup and a man was taking their photograph.

"This will be on the front cover of *Top Cats* magazine," said the man.

Mr Minted smirked. "Naturally," he said, "Selina is a top cat."

"She has won lots of trophies," said Mrs Minted, pointing to the cup.

Chip was impressed. It certainly would be nice to be a top cat like Selina and have a trophy.

At that moment, Mum leaned out of the kitchen window. She held up the teapot to Sue, Gary and Dad.

"Fancy a cup, anyone?" she called.

The robodog's ears swung up.

A cup? Yes, he
would definitely
like a cup!

He dashed into the kitchen.

Mum had just laid
out the cups and
saucers.

Chip jumped on to a chair. He put his paws on the table as Sue, Gary and Dad came in.

Mum grinned at Chip. "Fancy a cup, do you?" she asked.

Chip did. To everyone's surprise he took hold of one of the empty cups by the handle. Jumping off the chair he scampered out of the door.

"What's he up to?" cried Gary, as they all followed Chip into the garden.

The robodog dashed through the
gap in the fence. Dropping the
teacup at the photographer's feet, he
looked up with a grin.

The startled photographer stepped
back.
"What's going on?" he cried. "This
walking computer thingy has
brought me a cup!"

Mr Minted let out a snort of laughter as Mum, Dad, Sue and Gary arrived.

"Ha ha!" he cried. "Your silly home-made dog is all confused!

He wants to be like Selina and have his picture taken with a cup. A teacup!"

He hooted with laughter again and his wife tittered.

The robodog was puzzled. What was wrong with a teacup? It was still a cup, wasn't it?

Mr Minted waved the trophy under Chip's nose.

"It's a silver cup you want. Like this one," he sneered.

"But, of course, you'll never get one because you're not a cat, are you? Ha ha!"

Chip frowned. Was he a cat or wasn't he? He couldn't remember. He was feeling mixed up. He opened his mouth. "Miaow!" he said.

"Not again," groaned Dad.

"Why did he say *miaow*?" murmured Sue.

"He's all muddled, that's why," sneered Mr Minted.

"What you've got there is a dog who's *not* a dog, who thinks he's a *cat*!"

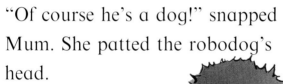

"Of course he's a dog!" snapped Mum. She patted the robodog's head.

"Show them how good a dog you are, Chip," she said. "Do something doggish."

Chip rubbed his back
against Mum's legs
and purred.
"Miaow," he said.

"Ha ha ha!" roared Mr and Mrs
Minted. "What a laugh!"

Sue, Gary and Dad went back to the house with Chip.

Mum went straight to her workshop to check the robodog's computer plan.

In the front room, Chip lay along
the back of the sofa, purring.
"What's got into you?"
asked Sue. "You're a
dog, not a cat."

"Yes, come on, Chip," said Gary.
"Start behaving
like a dog
again."

Chip stopped purring. A dog.
Yes … he should be behaving like a
dog. But how? He had forgotten.

His dog-
behaviour
circuits were
well and
truly mixed
up by now.

He started purring again. "Oh,
Chip!" groaned Sue and Gary.

"Don't worry," said Dad. "Your mum will sort him out."

He sipped his tea and began to read the newspaper.

"Look at this," he said. "Here's an article about the Roman ruins that are being excavated near here."

He pointed to a headline.

LAST DAY OF DIG
NOTHING FOUND YET

"We visited the dig with our class," said Sue. "It was great. The museum people showed us around."

"It's a shame they didn't find anything," said Gary. "All that digging for nothing."

The robodog's ears
swung up. Digging!
Wasn't that something
that dogs did?
Something that he
should do?

But how was he
supposed to do it?
He'd forgotten.

Perhaps he should go to the Roman
ruins. The museum people might
show him how to dig. Then he could
be a dog again.

Yes! That
was it!

38

He leaped off the sofa and rushed
out of the door.

"Chip!" cried Gary and Sue as they
dashed after him.

"Come back!"

They ran hard but the robodog was
so fast, he soon left them far behind.

Chip streaked along the street …

zoomed
around
corners …

and arrived at the dig a few minutes
later.

But the people from the museum
weren't digging. They were peering
into the end of an old pipe and
looking worried.

"There's a cat in that pipe," said
one. "And it won't come out."

"Perhaps it's stuck," said another. "We can't leave it there," said someone else. "What can we do?"

Chip walked forward and everyone gasped.

"What's this?" they cried. "Is it a robot dog?"

Chip frowned. If the
museum people
weren't sure he was
a dog then
maybe he was a
cat after all.
Perhaps he should speak
to another cat about it?

He put his nose into the end of
the pipe and let out a
loud "Miaow!"

From inside the pipe came a faint
reply …

"Miaow!" called Chip again, and
this time the reply was louder …

And suddenly … the cat came out,
blinking in the sunlight, curious to
know who the other cat was.

The museum people cheered.
Chip grinned and miaowed again in
a friendly how-are-you? kind of
way.

The cat took one look at the robodog and arched its back. "Sssss!" it hissed and flashed out a paw, hitting Chip right on the nose.

The cat ran off and Chip, startled, blinked in complete surprise.

The cat had hit him! Why?

Then suddenly it all came back to him. He was a dog – that's why! He was Chip, the robodog! And what did dogs like to do? They liked to dig. So Chip started digging. Dirt flew everywhere.

The museum people were horrified. "You can't dig like that!" they yelled. "You'll ruin the ruins!"

Gary and Sue arrived in the nick of time. They apologized to the museum people and led the robodog away.

"At least it's nice to see you're behaving like a dog again," whispered Gary.

48

"Yes," murmured Sue. "But what was all that cat business about?"

Suddenly Chip stopped and his super-sniff nose sensors twitched.

They had detected something interesting in the ground near by.

He dashed away and began to dig
again.
"Chip!" cried Sue.
"You're not supposed to
do that!"

"Hey!" yelled one
of the museum
people. "Stop
that!"

Everyone came running, but by the
time they all reached him, Chip had
dug a big hole.

The robodog looked up at them and grinned.

"Fancy a cup, anyone?" he said.

"Wh-what did he say?" stammered the museum people.

Chip grinned again. "Fancy a cup, do you?" he said and touched something with his paw.

They all stared into the hole. There, at Chip's feet, was a metal object. Carefully, one of the museum people lifted it out and gently brushed away the dirt.

Everyone gasped.

It was a beautiful silver
Roman cup!

The people from the museum were
thrilled. "This will be called 'The
Robodog Cup' and have a special
place in the museum!" they said.

A photographer arrived and took Chip's picture. She said it would be on the front page of the newspaper.

Chip didn't understand what all the fuss was about. After all, only cats liked getting silver cups and he was a dog.

Back home, Mum had discovered that Chip's computer programme needed a little adjustment. "That's why his behaviour got mixed up," she said.

She pressed some buttons on a remote control. Sue and Gary heard Chip's computer whirr and click.

"That's it," said Mum. "There shouldn't be any more problems."

Sue and Gary patted the robodog. "We'll make sure that Chip never forgets he's a dog again," said Sue.

"Yes," agreed Gary. "We'll play fetch and catch, teach him tricks and take him for walks."

Everyone looked happy except Dad.
He was gazing up at the new nest
box he had made.

"The blue tits
have gone," he
said sadly.

"It looks like my nest box will not
be used this year."

The robodog glanced into the sky. It was empty. He lifted up his muzzle. "Tee-tee!" he cried. "Tee-tee! Tee-tee! Tee-tee!"

It sounded exactly like the blue tits, and a moment later two appeared in the garden. They flew round the tree a few times and then ...

one after another, they popped into the nest box.

Dad was delighted.

"Brilliant!" he cried and patted the robodog.

"Thanks, Chip!
You're a marvel."

Sue and Gary were worried.

"I hope this doesn't mean that Chip thinks he's a bird now?" said Sue.

"Do you, Chip?" asked Gary.

59

Chip grinned and bounced on his springy legs.

"Woof!" he said.